MW01222028

Murder by bear
And Other Short Stories

Marlow Kelly

ISBN: 978-0-9952301-0-1

DEDICATION

To my family who drive me mad and keep me sane at the same time.

Murder by Bear was my first attempt at writing fiction and as such holds a special place

in my heart.

MURDER BY BEAR

Julia Hepburn crouched in the snow, peering over the barrel of a modified rifle. Where had she gone wrong? She was a nice, middle-class accountant from Toronto, not a hunter. Maybe, she hadn't made the best choices lately, and those choices resulted with her kneeling in a snowdrift on the outskirts of Churchill, Manitoba, waiting for a polar bear.

The move to Churchill was the latest in a long list of bad decisions. The people were great, but she was a city girl at heart. She enjoyed wearing her favorite black, patent, high-heel shoes on a daily basis, and reveled in starting each day with a skinny latte from a trendy coffee shop. Those things did not fit in with the remote lifestyle of Northern Canada.

She'd only agreed to relocate to the North because of her husband, Mike's persistence. He'd received a promotion with the Royal Canadian Mounted Police, which was contingent on him moving to Churchill. He'd used every piece of ammunition at his disposal to persuade her to join him. First he pouted, and then he charmed. When that failed, he talked about the babies he knew she wanted. Eventually, he wore her down. So she packed her designer clothes into boxes, put them in storage, and then purchased a warm, practical, down-filled coat.

Her ankles cramped. She stood, and stretched her legs. This polar bear hunt was another of Mike's bright ideas. Every autumn, between August, and November the omnivores migrated to the Churchill area while they waited for the sea to freeze. Some of them scavenged for food too close to town and had to be sedated and relocated.

When Mike asked her to help with the hunt she had refused. What did she know about tranquilizer darts, guns and hunting? But, once again, he'd worn her down.

Jake, the hunt coordinator strode toward her. A conservation officer, he was tall with broad shoulders, and no hint of a middle-aged spread, which was a surprise given he was nearing fifty.

"Are you ready for this?" His eyes narrowed, scrutinizing her.

"I don't know." She bit her lip, and then patted her mouth, hoping the damp skin wouldn't freeze. The nervous habit always irritated Mike.

"You don't have to take part. You can wait in my truck if you want."

She glanced at her husband a hundred yards away. His striking features animated as he talked to the other hunters. He was so eager for them to fit in, and helping to rid the community of a nuisance bear would go a long way toward their acceptance. "No, I'll do it."

"It's okay to be scared." His grey hair lifted in the frigid breeze.

She sucked in a breath and straightened her spine. "I'm not scared, really. I've just been a little accident-prone lately."

"I heard you almost burned the house down." His brow wrinkled.

"I don't understand how it happened. I wasn't using the space heater, and I never put it near the curtains."

"Was anything damaged?"

"Everything. By the time I woke up the whole house was full of smoke. All our stuff reeks." She turned her gaze to the snowy landscape, and winced, wishing she had sunglasses to guard against the glare.

"Where was Mike when all this happened?"

"He was at work."

"It was lucky you woke when you did."

"Yes, the neighbors were banging on the door. That's what saved me." She gave a little shiver as she remembered her close call.

"But one incident doesn't make you accident-prone."

"Yesterday, I nearly electrocuted myself."

"How?" His eyes widened.

"When I plugged in my hairdryer I got a zap that threw me across the room."

"Are you okay?"

"Yes, but I swear my heart stopped, then started again." Her hand went to her chest, as she remembered the all-consuming pain of the electric shock.

"I can see why you're a little nervous."

"I'm probably being silly."

"Don't worry. I'll only be twenty-five yards from you. Have you loaded the tranquilizers into the rifle?"

"I don't know much about that kind of thing so Mike did it for me."

Jake's radio crackled. He held it to his ear, and then said, "It's time. Are you sure you're ready?"

She nodded, and he strode away.

Once again, she crouched behind the snow bank, and stared out over the Arctic Tundra.

At last, the bear appeared, a white, shifting outline. Her skin tingled with a mixture of fear and excitement as he came into view. He walked with a steady gait, his enormous paws spreading as he moved, giving the impression of a large, overgrown puppy, instead of the dangerous beast she knew him to be. He sniffed the air, and then as if catching a scent, changed direction, and headed straight for her. She steadied her firearm, preparing to shoot.

The sound of helicopter blades cut through the frozen sky. The bear panicked, and charged. She took aim, and shot. The tranquilizer dart hit his neck. He did not stop, did not slow. Terror surged through her as she lifted the rifle to her shoulder and fired again. The second dart had less effect than the first.

Her mind flashed to Mike loading her rifle, and in her heart she knew it was useless. He had used the bear to murder her. Her recent accidents were attempts on her life.

It was too late to run. Too late to do anything but pray. In her peripheral vision she caught a glimpse of a figure aiming a gun, another dart struck the bear. The beast went limp midstride. His body smacked the ground, forcing the air out of his lungs with a hiss.

She stood frozen to the spot, watching as the helicopter landed, and men surrounded the huge animal. They checked its vitals, and then rolled it onto a net.

"Are you okay?" Jake stood beside her.

She hadn't heard him approach, hadn't noticed anything but the bear. "Three darts, it took three darts."

"Yes, it did. You were great. You didn't lose your nerve and start running."

"Three darts," she repeated.

"I'm really surprised the first two didn't work. There must be something wrong with your tranquilizers."

Julia glared at Mike, who stood on the other side of the net watching her. Hate flickered in his dark brown eyes. Then he turned his back to her, and struck up a conversation with the man standing next to him. At that moment she knew beyond a doubt, he had tried to kill her. She put her nose to her jacket, and sniffed. Had he laced her clothes with scent to attract the bear? Probably. Meticulous by nature, he wouldn't have left anything to chance. She had no idea why he wanted her dead, but she couldn't go home with him.

She raced to catch Jake as he boarded the helicopter.

"What are you going to do with the bear now?" she shouted above the roar of the blades.

"We're going to airlift him to a bay that's about twenty-five kilometers up the coast."

"Can I come, and watch? I won't get in the way."

He shrugged. "Why not? You've earned it."

She climbed into the back seat not bothering to say goodbye to her husband.

Once airborne, she looked down to see Mike standing below, watching her leave. Did he have another plot to end her life? Was he going home now to put his plan into action? She hoped so.

Once home, he would open the front door, and before he had a chance to smell the gas, he would turn on the light. Hopefully, the explosion would kill him. The small wrench she had used to tamper with the gas line lay deep in her pocket. She would dispose of it while the others were busy dropping off the bear.

When he had urged her to go on the bear hunt she'd suspected he was going to make another attempt on her life. If her suspicions had proved unfounded she would have gone home with him, and saved him.

Marrying Mike was the worst decision she had ever made, but it was a bad decision she wouldn't have to live with anymore.

I've always been fascinated with the idea that our assessment of the truth isn't so much about fact but rather our own flawed perception of reality.

<u>Escape</u>

Marilee sat at her green vinyl table tallying her meager collection of dimes and nickels. She licked her lips as she counted. She'd wanted coffee with cream since the moment she'd dragged her sleepy body out of bed. The craving was so strong she could almost taste the rich, velvety drink.

She finished counting, pounded the table with her fist, and leaned back in her rickety folding chair. Yes, she had enough to buy a small carton. She hadn't indulged in the delicious luxury in weeks. She'd relocated to the small town of Trout Lake, in the Kootenay Mountains of British Columbia, two months ago. And was lucky enough to find a home where she could live off-the-grid, but the hand to mouth existence eroded her self-esteem, making her wonder if she'd made the right decision.

The interior of the grim little log cabin was dark, musty, and empty except for the old creaky metal-frame bed, and a faded, vinyl, patio table. Her temporary home wasn't much to look at, but it was dry, warm, vermin-free, and safe – for now.

Using a small cracked mirror she checked her appearance. She had bathed in a nearby mountain stream this morning, using some of her precious soap. The water was so frigid she was forced to rush, not allowing herself to remember hot showers, and fluffy towels. Her long mane of auburn hair was gone, replaced with a short practical bob. She shrugged, placed the mirror face down on the table, and dismissed her reflection.

"It doesn't matter." How many times had she said those words in the last two months? *It doesn't matter* was a mantra she'd told herself every time she stuffed her legs into the threadbare jeans she'd purchased at the thrift store, or spotted someone wearing clothes with designer labels—labels with which she was all too familiar. That life was in the past. These days she worked at being inconspicuous, a woman who blended into her surroundings.

There was a chance her husband, Brandon, would hunt her down. She had done everything to cover her tracks, but what if she'd left a clue, a small crumb he could follow? No, she'd come to this remote location, because he wouldn't expect her to live in the country. But what if—

She stood, not allowing herself to go down that path. Replaying the past wouldn't do any good.

Stuffing the change into her pocket, she stepped outside, squinting in the bright mid-morning sun. A wall of heat hit her like a body blow. It wasn't yet noon, and the temperature was already oppressive. She quickened her pace, hoping to make it to town before the stifling temperatures made hiking on the winding, mountain highway unbearable.

Jack Sweeney, a local rancher, and her landlord, pulled up beside her in his new, red pickup truck. He rolled down the window and smiled. His light grey eyes intense as he took in every detail of her appearance. "Need a ride? I'm heading into town."

Part of her wanted to refuse. She didn't want to get in his vehicle. She didn't want to talk to him. He was too curious, too attentive. She glanced at the heat shimmering off the highway. The blistering temperature made walking impractical, and she'd seem rude if she didn't accept.

"If it's no bother," she said, looking at the road, the ground, anywhere, but him.

He stretched across the truck, and opened the passenger door. "Hop in. Where're you heading?"

"Hopkins store." The General Store was the one-stop-shop for Trout Lake. An old-fashioned merchant where you could buy milk, nails, and catch up on town gossip. Marilee climbed onto the luxurious leather seat.

The muscles of his arms flexed under his tanned skin, as he nudged back his wide-brimmed cowboy hat. "How many times do I have to tell you, you don't have to be scared of me? You're safe here. In Trout Lake we look after our own."

She gave him a small smile, and then turned to look at the scenery. "You're kind. I guess it'll take time."

Jack swore under his breath. "It breaks my heart to see a woman's spirit crushed."

She didn't reply. It wasn't a comment that required an answer.

"I know you've never said anything, but word is your husband abused you, and you're hiding out."

Marilee schooled her features, hoping her emotions didn't show on her face. "You've been talking about me?"

"You're a new face in a small town, there's bound to be talk."

Her heart stopped. Perhaps coming to a community with only two hundred people wasn't such a great idea. She should have stayed in Calgary where she would be one anonymous face among millions. No, remaining in the city hadn't been an option. Brandon's tentacles reached to every part of town from the mansions of Roxboro to the drug addled alleys of the downtown core. He would have found her if she'd stayed.

Jack pulled up in front of the store. Marilee scrambled out of the truck, waved goodbye, and darted inside.

She wasn't surprised to find the shop packed with chattering women. Hopkins was a communal meeting place. She ignored the crowd, and grabbed a tiny carton of cream from the glass, and steel fridge. As she made her way to the cash register the crowd hushed. A cold chill inched up her spine. Something was wrong, very wrong. She'd worked hard at being invisible, but had made a fundamental mistake by moving here. She saw that now. Everyone knew everyone else's business in a small town, and a woman who lived off-the-grid in a tiny cabin was bound to be a curiosity.

Mrs. Hopkins, a rail thin woman with white hair, broke the silence. "Marilee, I should tell you there was a man in here thirty minutes ago saying terrible things about you."

"What man? What things?" Her legs weakened, and her knees threatened to buckle. She leaned against the counter for support.

"He said he was your husband, and you had stolen half a million dollars from him."

"He's here." Her vision blurred, and for a moment she thought she might faint. She inhaled through her nose, held her breath for the count of eight, and then released the air through her mouth. She wanted to turn, and run, but her legs wouldn't cooperate.

"We don't believe a word of it, do we ladies?" Mrs. Hopkins announced. A chorus of agreement echoed around the room.

"No, if that were true the police would be looking for me," Marilee said, more to herself than her audience.

"Oh, he said the police are investigating, and now he's found you, he'll make sure they come for you today."

"I have to get away." She mustered her strength, and took a step toward the door.

"Stop," Mrs. Hopkins ordered. "Running won't help, but I have a plan. I've called Jack. He's coming to pick you up. He'll drive you back to your cabin where you will collect all your things. There is to be no evidence once you are done. Do you understand?"

"You're going to help me?"

"Of course. Once you have your belongings Jack will drive you back to town. We'll transfer you from house to house as needed. The first night you will stay with Thelma." Mrs. Hopkins pointed to a rather portly, grey haired woman, standing by her side. "And in the mean time, we will introduce him to the art of misdirection."

The art of misdirection. Who was this woman? Had Mrs. Hopkins secretly run black ops? Or maybe she'd read too many spy novels? If Marilee had to guess she would have said it was the novels. "That's kind of you, but—"

"There's Jack outside. Go."

Marilee ran. As she reached the truck a large hand seized her wrist.

"Hello Monica, it's so nice to see you again."

She bit back a scream, and prayed for composure as she turned to face Brandon, the man who had once been her husband.

"What have you done with my money?" Spittle gathered at the corners of his mouth as his handsome features twisted with rage. He wore a white designer shirt that stretched across his wide shoulders. Marilee knew he worked out every day in order to keep his physique toned, fit, and strong.

Maybe if she reasoned with him. "I don't know what—"

"Don't say another word. Everything that comes out of your mouth is a lie. So don't bother trying to deny you stole half a million dollars from me because I know you did. I also know Monica isn't your real name."

A brown stick flashed between them as a loud smack sounded. Brandon yelped, released Marilee, and jumped back, clutching his injured arm.

Mrs. Hopkins held a broom handle like a baseball bat, ready to strike again. "Don't touch her, you good for nothing louse."

"You don't understand. She's a thief. She stole my money." Brandon took another step back.

"You're just saying that to get her back. We all know you beat her." The older woman moved to stand between Marilee, and Brandon.

"What?" His eye's widened, and his mouth fell open.

Jack honked the horn. "Get in."

Marilee dived into the pickup, landing in a jumbled mess. She struggled to put on her seatbelt as Jack hit the gas.

"I'll take you to my place," Jack said.

"No, I want to go back to my cabin." She turned to see her ex-husband surrounded by a pack of angry women. "I hope they don't kill him."

"He'll be a bit bruised, but he'll know better than to come here, and try and take you."

"You're very kind, but what if he really did call the police? Won't you get into trouble for helping me?"

"You let me worry about that. Thelma has a son on the force. I'll call him, and we'll get this loser sorted out."

"Thank you." Marilee put a hand to her chest in an attempt to calm her racing heart.

He came to a stop in front of the cabin. "Grab whatever you need. I'll be back in fifteen minutes."

"Where are you going?"

"To get my rifle, just in case there's trouble. I won't be long."

Marilee waited until the truck drove away, before she marched into the dark, cool interior. It was time to leave.

She went straight to the bed, groped under the mattress, and plucked out a set of keys. Then, she headed to the back of the property. As soon as she reached the cover of the forest she broke into a run, hoping to make it to the next valley before nightfall.

The sun hung low on the western horizon when she arrived at the clearing near the narrow, paved road. There was just enough light left for her to find the motorbike in the undergrowth. She dragged the Harley out, and checked to make sure everything was in working order.

Then she searched for the hollow tree where she'd hidden her things, and yanked out three plastic, garbage bags. The first two contained her helmet, and leathers. These were invaluable to her escape. If she travelled by car someone might be able to give her description to the police, but her bike gear concealed her physical appearance. A passer-by would be hard pressed to describe anything about her.

She turned her attention to the third plastic bag. It contained a leather saddlebag. Undoing the clasp, she checked to make sure her fake ID, and money were still there.

She almost felt sorry for Brandon...almost. He'd lied when he'd accused her of stealing half a million dollars. She'd stolen closer to one million.

She shook her head and climbed on the bike. The good people of Trout Lake had assumed she'd been abused, but she'd never said so, she just kept her eyes down, and her mouth shut. Their collective imagination had done the rest. It was almost a shame to go, where else would she find a whole town just waiting to be fleeced, but she couldn't stay. Brandon was sleazy when it came to his business practices so there was a good chance the money was already stolen, and he hadn't contacted the authorities. But Jack was a straight arrow, a man who said exactly what he meant, and he would call the police. Once they investigated they'd find she operated under a long list of aliases, and had left a trail of marks in her wake.

She steered the bike onto the highway, heading for Vancouver. Once there, she would dye her hair blonde, get some extensions, and become Brittany Lamoure. A woman who wore short skirts, low cut tops, and liked sugar daddies. She laughed as the bike roared up the highway. Tomorrow she would definitely have cream in her coffee.

This piece of flash fiction was written in response to a challenge from a fellow author.
Write a story with a beginning, middle and end in five hundred words or less

THE ENCOUNTER

1838 London, England

Emily scanned the faces in the crowd. The streets were lined with people waiting for Queen Victoria's coronation carriage, but Emily's gentleman was not there. It was important she meet him. He could provide enough money for mama to see a doctor, and be their ticket out of the city.

Consumption had overwhelmed her mother in recent weeks, causing her health to diminish. So when mama had insisted on this last meeting; Emily had been unable to refuse, but she had her misgivings. After all, he was probably a man with a wife, and children, and what she was doing was wrong.

The crowd surged, and a wall of people pressed against her. She struggled to escape the wave of bodies that dragged her in their wake. Suddenly, a hand grabbed hers, and pulled her free.

She found herself facing a tall man with smiling, green eyes. He wore a jacket that had seen better days, and a shirt that showed signs of wear. Normally, she would stay, and flirt, glad of his company, but today she had other responsibilities.

"Hello." He bowed, and kissed her hand. "It's not every day I get to save a beautiful damsel in distress. How may I be of service?"

He stood straight, and her breath caught at the sight of his broad shoulders and dark, wavy hair that curled around his collar.

Reluctantly, she pulled her hand from his. "I have to go. I promised my mother."

She spun on her heel, and ran away from the crowd toward the market at Covent Garden. Where could her gentleman be? The marketplace was loud and raucous, as proprietors hollered their prices to passers-by. She darted between stalls, wondering what could have happened to him. And then he appeared, directly in front of her.

He had not noticed her yet because he was distracted by the tobacco stand. He was exactly as she imagined—middle-aged, with a distinguished moustache, wearing an exquisitely tailored suit. Emily smiled as she watched him flick a speck of dirt from his shoulder. Everything about him indicated wealth and privilege, from his clothes to his polished, leather boots.

Someone knocked her elbow, awakening her from her trance. She dashed toward him, and was almost there when her foot hit a stone. She flew forward. Her arms grabbed him about the waist as she tried to right herself.

He helped her to her feet, and tipped his hat in apology. She nodded politely, and continued on her way, clutching his billfold in her hand. She smiled as she headed home. Mama would be so pleased.

Mothering Sunday was celebrated in England as early as the 17th century. It was held on the fourth Sunday of lent and was a day when everyone returned to their "mother" church.
This short Mother's Day story is dedicated to caring, loving and conniving mothers everywhere.

FIRST IMPRESSIONS

Berkshire, England
Mothering Sunday, 2nd April 1905

Ann Hamilton sat in her parent's brougham carriage, staring at the forbidding grey stone façade of Hendon Hall. It was an impressive structure with roman columns, a multitude of sash windows, and a summerhouse in the side garden. The manor and grounds were the epitome of wealth and prosperity.

Ann hated it on sight. For all its elegance, Hendon Hall might as well be Newgate Prison, and she a convict awaiting the noose.

"You have to make a good impression. We are counting on you." Her mother's high pitched, nasal voice vibrated in the close confines of the carriage.

"Mother, I'm not sure if—"

"I know, I know, it's not your fault. Why on earth your father would mortgage us to the hilt, and borrow money from a callous man like Lord Brightman is beyond me. But if you don't agree to marry their son we will be out on the streets. Is that what you want?"

Ann wondered if Lady Brightman would examine her the way a horse breeder might inspect a mare. She had visions of an old lady with white hair inspecting her teeth, and asking about colic.

Not that it mattered, because this plan would never work. Ann's mother was an imaginative woman who tended to picture the world as if it were a story from her ladies magazine. But Ann, like her father, had a gift for seeing the realities of life, without the benefit of illusion. And she saw herself as a plain, brown-haired woman who was not remarkable in any way.

"Look at me, Mother. He's not going to want to marry—"

"Nonsense. You're pretty enough, when you hold your head up and don't slouch. Remember, you're as good as the next girl; just mind your manners, and things will go swimmingly." Her mother climbed out of the carriage.

Ann followed, wishing she could garner an ounce of her mother's enthusiasm for this venture. Her future, indeed, her family's future, dangled in the hands of a mysterious individual, Lord Brightman's son. What if he hated the very sight of her? Or was covered in boils? Or took to drink? What if he were cruel? No, surely her father would find another way rather than marry her off to a brute?

She put a hand to her stomach, but couldn't prevent it from rolling. She struggled to inhale, but her restrictive clothing hampered her breathing. Mother insisted she wear the latest fashion. Her corset extended from her bust to her hips, and was covered by a burgundy silk day dress, accentuated with delicate Irish lace. She felt like a doll at a tea party.

She bent her head as she dragged her feet, wishing she were home at Holbourne Manor, sitting in the garden with a sketchbook and pencil in hand.

"Come along, Ann, don't dawdle," her mother snapped, interrupting her thoughts, as they entered a grand drawing room, tastefully decorated in pale blue with white trim.

"Mrs. Hamilton, it's nice to see you." Lady Brightman smiled.

Lady Brightman wasn't at all as Ann had imagined. She was statuesque with coifed brown hair and large, blue, smiling eyes. "George is anxious to meet your lovely daughter." She waved a hand toward a young man, seated by the fire.

Unlike his mother, there was nothing remarkable about George's appearance. He was plain with dark hair and glasses. He did not stand and greet them. Instead, he sat with his back straight and glared at her over the rim of his spectacles. Ann ignored the slight, deciding to play the gracious guest.

Her mother and Lady Brightman sat on a blue velvet settee.

"Please sit down." Her hostess pointed to a matching chair near George.

Anne curtsied, and strode to the chair. Unfortunately, she misjudged the placement of her seat, and landed with only part of her behind on the cushion. She threw her arms out trying to grasp something, anything, to stop her fall. But there was nothing to grab. She crashed to the floor with her legs in the air, her skirt covering her face.

"Oh no," her mother cried.

Ann's face burned. She struggled to a sitting position, scrambling to cover her legs. "That was inelegant," she said, trying to make light of the situation.

George gave her a cold stare, and then rose to his feet.

Maybe he would come to her aid, and play the gentlemen.

He turned his back, and stalked to the window in an obvious show of contempt.

How dare he? Yes, she'd been inept and graceless. But she hadn't meant to embarrass herself or those in her company. He, on the other hand, was just plain rude. He could have chosen to be a courteous host, but instead he'd decided to embarrass her further with his disdain. What would life be like once they were married? Her days with George Brightman would be filled with misery. A pulse throbbed through her head, and her stomach lurched. Her worst fears had come to fruition. Her husband-to-be was a rude, mean-spirited swine.

****

Tuesday, 4th April 1905

Ann sat with her hands clasped in her lap, and her eyes cast down. She'd been given strict instructions to stay seated. Her mother had invited George and Lady Brightman for afternoon tea. Why they continued with this amicable charade was beyond her. She knew everything she needed to know about the younger Brightman.

Once everyone had eaten their fill of cucumber sandwiches, and Devonshire scones, Ann's mother addressed Lady Brightman. "Amelia, let's take a turn about the garden, and leave these two to get to know each other."

Ann shot to her feet. "Mother, that's just not done. You—"

"You have so much to learn about each other. George, do tell Ann about your work, and where you will live once you are married." Lady Brightman looped her arm through Mrs. Hamilton's "Come along, Emily."

They strolled out of the room arm-in-arm.

A young single woman was never left alone in the company of a man. Would George think her a Trollope? She put her hands to her face in an effort to cool her burning cheeks, and walked to the window, horrified at her mother's behavior. "I-I-have to apologize…"

His breath tickled the back of her neck, making her jump. How had he gotten across the room without her hearing him?

"You won't get what you want by marrying me," he whispered.

"And what do I want?" She turned to face him.

"Money. I don't have any, and I never will." He inched closer so their toes were touching, his long legs pressing against her skirts. "Are you going to let me kiss you?" His breath warmed her neck.

"I never—"

He ran his finger across her lower lip. Her tongue darted out to quell her reaction to his touch. She became aware of his form; his long legs, the breadth of his shoulders, his glossy, dark hair. She tilted her head, only to be captured by his cold, hard gaze. He hated her. That notion hit her like a slap to the face. He was mad at her. How dare he? She was the one who'd been thrust into this appalling situation.

He bent his head. Did he believe her a strumpet? Was he going to kiss her? She turned her face away.

"Do you honestly think I will treat you like a lady after everything your family has done to force me into this marriage?" He gave a hard, cold chuckle.

Without thinking, she kicked his shin. He yelped, and stepped back, clutching his leg.

She stomped down on his foot. "How dare you?" she spat. "You have no right to judge me. If your father hadn't threatened to make my parents homeless, I would not be forced to marry a pompous twit like you. And don't worry, after we're married I will continue to live with my mother." She stormed out of the room, praying she'd seen the last of George Brightman.

****

Wednesday 5th April 1905

Ann tugged the blanket tighter around her body as she sat in her parent's garden, sketching a hedgehog. Her sleep-deprived mind was so muddled she'd forgotten her coat. Mornings in the summer should be warm with sunshine, but the weather resembled her mood—gloomy, and miserable.

She penciled even strokes across the page, as she alternated between misery and anger. Misery because she had to marry George, and anger because he thought her a jezebel who wanted his money. The only solace she could find was in her art, and the woodland creatures she loved to draw.

A hand touched her shoulder. She jumped, and turned to face her visitor. George. Had he come to insult her again? Her eyes watered. No, she wasn't going to cry, not in front of him. She would send him on his way, and then escape to her room. "Go away, George"

"I—"

"I don't want you here," she snapped. This was her sanctuary, her refuge.

He walked around the bench and knelt before her. "Please accept my apology."

"Apology? Is this a trick?" There had to be a catch. He hated her, and she detested him.

He gave a great sigh that made him seem more like a small boy than a grown man. "Until your outburst I was led to believe this marriage was all your doing. I thought you were after my title, and I resented being forced.

17

But after you kicked me in the shin," he rubbed his leg, "which I deserved by the way, I asked Mother to tell me the truth."

"What did she say?"

"Father will cut my allowance if I don't marry you. I won't receive a penny."

She narrowed her eyes. Surely as a man he would have some say, some way to avoid this marriage. "And working for a living is obviously out of the question?"

"Oh, I work, but I don't earn enough to pay for my accommodation and food." He rose, and sat beside her.

"I have no interest in your title or your money. I'm quite content to live my days as a spinster."

"But you are being forced—"

"Yes, but that is the fate of a woman. We are at the whim of others. You're a man. You don't have to submit to such demands."

He frowned. "I do if I want to continue my work."

"Can't you do something else for a living?"

"I'd rather marry you, especially if you're going to stay with your mother." He gave her a small smile.

"What?"

"Think about it. We could get married, you can stay here, and I can go back to my work, categorizing the plants, and animals of the Fens in East Anglia." His eyes shone.

"I've heard the Fens are wild and mysterious," Ann said, surprised at the hint of wonder she heard in her own voice.

"I don't know about mysterious, but they are wild. The untouched portions are teeming with wildlife." For the first time since she'd met him he seemed animated and alive.

"What kind of wildlife?"

"In the waterways you'll find otters and voles. In the summer there's a lively assortment of butterflies, including the swallowtail."

"What else?" She enjoyed his infectious enthusiasm.

"Let me see, there are reed warblers, marsh tits, cuckoos, nightingales, oh, and long-eared owls. It's always a treat when I spot one of those."

"And that's all you do all day, wander the marsh and look at birds and animals." No wonder he didn't earn any money.

"No, I observe them, and write down everything I see. What they eat, nesting habits, mating rituals, and that sort of thing. The Fens are being drained to make farmland. I'm scared one day they will be gone. Do you know beavers used to live there, but they were hunted to extinction? I'm trying to catalogue the plants, and animals before they disappear." He took off his glasses and rubbed his eyes.

"So you draw—"

"I try, although my skill as an artist is lacking." He gave her a lopsided smile.

"The Fens sound wonderful."

His eyes were the most stunning shade of blue she had ever seen. Why hadn't she noticed them before? And he liked animals. Could her first impression be wrong, or was he only being nice for his own ends?

"I am sorry for my behavior, and my family's role in all this." He took her hand in his. "Marry me, for your family's sake as well as mine. You will be free to pursue your own interests. I won't make any demands on you."

She searched his face for any signs of deceit, but found none. But there again, she didn't know him well enough to know if he was proficient at lying. She turned his palm. It was calloused and rough, not what she'd expect from the son of a lord.

"So if I want to spend my time drawing you won't object?"

"No," he smiled. A lock of dark hair fell across his brow. He really was handsome in a bookish way.

"Will I be called on to attend social functions?"

"If you want to, I'll even escort you, but please don't ask me to attend more than one a month. I really—"

"And if I want to live with my mother after we are married?"

"I won't object. Why would I? My life will be unchanged."

The hedgehog she had been sketching, scurried back into the bushes, probably returning to its den. Maybe, being married to George wouldn't be so bad.

"May I." He turned her sketchpad so he could examine her work. "You are an accomplished artist."

"Oh, I don't—"

"Would you consider coming to the Fens to draw the great spotted kingfisher? I've tried to capture its likeness, but don't seem to be able to do it justice."

"I'd be happy to…after we are married. It wouldn't be appropriate—"

"Then you will be my wife?"

"George, I was always going to marry you. I have no choice."

****

Wicken Fen, Cambridgeshire, England
2nd December 1905

Ann sat by the fire in the cozy cottage she shared with her husband, enjoying a soothing cup of tea. The incessant drum of rain on the slate roof lulled her. She stretched, and lay down on the settee using George's legs as a pillow.

"How's our child today?" He ran his hand over her stomach, as their baby kicked.

"Happy." At five months it was an active baby, who liked nothing more than to tap his feet, especially at night when Ann was trying to sleep.

Normally, she enjoyed talking about her pregnancy, but today she had something important to discuss. She removed an envelope from her skirt pocket. "The last time I wrote to Father, I was impertinent enough to suggest he not borrow any money as he doesn't have any more children to marry off, and today I received an interesting reply."

George's eyes widened. "What did he say?"

"He didn't know what I was talking about. He hasn't borrowed money in twenty years. Apparently, my grandfather left him a fortune. Although he's pleased I am married to the son of mother's closest friend."

"Are you suggesting our mothers—?"

"Lied to us."

"To be honest, I'm not surprised."

"You're not? George Brightman, what aren't you telling me?"

"I probably should have mentioned this before." George shifted out from under her, and walked to the mantle. "I got a letter from the family solicitor to say my trust fund, which was set up by my grandfather, has increased my living allowance as I am about to turn thirty."

Ann sat up. "Do you mean to say your father could never have cut off your allowance?"

"That's right. I always had an income from my grandfather. I didn't need father's money."

"And no one told you?"

"No…well, maybe they did, and I forgot, but the fact is, Mother lied."

"They both did. I can't believe it. Our mothers tricked us into marriage."

"What do you think we should do about it?" he asked.

She touched her stomach. As much as she hated anyone to get the better of her, because of her mother's fib she had a loving husband, a fulfilling life, and in four months she would have a baby. Would she tell a lie to ensure her child's happiness?

She stood, and walked to her husband, putting her arms about his waist. "Sometimes we have to accept that mother knows best."

FBI Special Agent Finn Callaghan is a character from my upcoming novel, Sun Seeker, but he didn't begin his career in a resident agency in Montana.

The Wily Witness

From the files of Finn Callaghan

FBI Headquarters New York City, New York
25th July 2010, 8 a.m.

Finn glanced at the huge stack of files on his desk. He had a degree in criminology, ten years experience with the military police, top of his class at Quantico, and he was stuck doing filing in a world that was supposed to be going paperless.

Special Agent Nathan Levenson, Finn's mentor and partner, strong-armed a gangly teenager around the grey, chest-high cubicle walls that divided the twentieth floor of the Major Crimes Division.

"I didn't do it. I swear. Anna... I was there to see Anna, " the kid whimpered, his face pale.

"Don't you know it's a criminal offense to lie to a federal agent?" Levenson shoved him into a chair across the aisle from Finn's desk.

The youth fell silent, staring at the ground. He squirmed in his seat, but with his hands cuffed behind him, he couldn't seem to get comfortable. Eventually, he leant to one side in an attempt to accommodate the unnatural position.

"Anything I can do?" Finn asked, hoping for a reprieve from the stack of paperwork.

"No, as a probationary agent you can stick to what you're good at."

"Filing?"

"Exactly." Levenson smiled, rubbing a hand over his smooth, bald head.

Finn resisted the temptation to punch the smile from Nathan's face; instead he stood at his desk, and flicked through the stack of papers. There were at least six months worth of documents, all of them Levenson's. The special agent was obviously behind, and had decided to foist the work onto him, a junior agent.

Finn couldn't complain, not without torpedoing his own career. It was only his second day in the field. If he made a request for a different mentor he risked being labeled as difficult. He picked up the FD-395—advice of rights and waiver form—from the top of the pile. If he worked hard he might be finished by the end of the day, then tomorrow he could focus on some real work.

Levenson bent down so that his face was a hair's breadth from the teenager in front of him. "Kid, you just scaled three stories, disabled an alarmed window, and by-passed one of the most sophisticated security systems on the planet, because of a girl?"

"I didn't disable the alarm. Anna did, and she—"

"Save it for the judge."

"Judge?" More color drained from the youth's face.

"We have video of you climbing the building. The diamonds you took are worth five hundred thousand dollars? That's grand larceny in the second degree. It carries a sentence of up to fifteen years. Tell us where you hid the gems, and maybe the DA will cut you a deal."

"I didn't take any diamonds, I swear." The kid's Adam's apple bobbed. "I want to make a phone call."

"Good idea, call your lawyer. He'll tell you to cut a deal."

"I'm calling my Mom."

"You think your mommy can save you?"

"I'm sixteen. I've seen cop shows. A minor needs a guardian present. I want to call my mom. Now."

Levenson shrugged, and turned to Finn. "Watch him while I make the arrangements."

Nathan disappeared into the corner office of their superior, Senior Special Agent Mark Windham.

Finn strolled over to the young man across the aisle. He was lanky with a mild case of teenage acne, and a chunk of dark hair, which fell across large, hazel-green eyes.

"Hey kid, you got a name?"

"Noah Lewis." He had an open, animated face with a deep dimple on the left side.

"Have you ever been in trouble before?"

"I don't know anything about diamonds. I thought Anna would be there." Noah wrapped his ankles around the legs of the chair. Finn's classes at Quantico included reading non-verbal behaviors, instinctive responses caused by the limbic system. Agents analyzed these physical cues to assess the veracity of their suspects. The position of Noah's legs suggested a freeze response. By itself it didn't tell Finn much, except Noah was scared, but that was to be expected whether he was guilty or not.

"A girl, huh." Finn hoped he seemed relaxed, conversational. The more comfortable the subject, the easier it was to read his physical reactions. "Tell me about her."

"We've been dating in secret because her dad's strict—"

"Does she have a last name?"

"It's Zingel, Anna Zingel." Noah didn't squint or give any other negative response when he talked about her. An honest answer.

"Okay, so where do you go to meet Anna. I assume she's your age."

Noah nodded. "We meet in Bryant Park, near the statue of William Dodge."

"So why the change of venue?"

"She said her family would be out, and we could... you know...we were going to..." He blushed.

"Are you saying, you thought you were going to have sex with her?"

"Yeah." Noah nodded again, his cheeks a vibrant pink. "It's not illegal. We're both underage." His responses seemed candid and honest.

"Why did having sex with this girl involve climbing three stories, breaking, and entering?" Finn struggled to keep any hint of censure out of his voice. He needed Noah to be comfortable and forthcoming, not defensive about his poor choices.

"She lives in a secure building with cameras. She said her dad could play back and monitor the video, but if I climbed to her window he'd never know." He tilted his head away in an obvious show of discomfort.

Why? Was he embarrassed or lying? Finn leant against Levenson's desk, and folded his arms across his chest. "Where is her apartment?"

"It's on the corner of Fifth Avenue and Forty-Seventh Street."

"The one you climbed tonight?"

"That's right."

"Do you use ropes or climbing gear?"

"I don't need them." He stretched his legs out in front of him, comfortable with his achievement.

"So you free-climbed three floors in the Diamond District?"

"To meet Anna—"

"But it's the Diamond District. You must've realized you would be arrested?"

"No. I didn't think..." Noah's eyes widened, indicating surprise. He drew his legs together, and lowered his head, a common physical reflex to shame.

"Okay, so if you're meeting a girl, why break in through the third floor

23

window?"

Noah's head snapped up. "I didn't. The window was unlocked. I just opened it." He didn't squint, tilt away, or show any other sign of discomfort, which suggested he was telling the truth.

"Unlocked, huh. And when all the alarms sounded?"

He closed his eyes. Eye-blocking, it was an instinctive response to shut out a memory. Then he opened them, and shrugged—false bravado.

"So you climbed into the storeroom of Wolff Diamonds, then what?"

Noah squinted, and his pupils momentarily constricted. A negative response to the memory? Maybe. "I thought I'd got the wrong window. I didn't think I'd be accused of stealing. I don't have any diamonds. The other agent searched me."

No diamonds, interesting.

"We have video of you climbing the building. If you were meeting a girl why hasn't she come forward?" Levenson snapped.

Finn flinched at the sound of the senior agent's voice. *Damn.* He hadn't realized Nathan was behind him. Was he angry at Finn's interference? Probably.

He turned to his colleague, "Sorry, I didn't mean to step on your toes. Just curious."

"I get it. You're keen to prove yourself, but we do not interrogate suspects at my desk. We have an interview room, and procedures for that."

"Understood." Finn walked back to his desk. His own poor judgment baffled him. He'd been a law enforcement officer for ten years, and had built a reputation for being by the book. But as a captain with the military police he would've chewed out any officer who'd neglected to follow procedure when questioning a suspect. So why did he feel the need to break the rules now? Maybe the filing had addled his mind.

"And if you interfere with my investigation again I'll have your head." Levenson pointed a finger at Finn's chest.

Finn held up his hands in surrender. "It won't happen again."

Levenson grabbed Noah by the arm, and marched him toward the interview rooms.

Finn strode to his desk, grabbed a stack of filing, and rammed the pieces of paper into a hanging folder. He resented Levenson's decision to berate him in front of a suspect. The senior agent was angry, which was understandable, but that was no excuse for being disrespectful.

Were Finn's personal feelings getting in the way of his judgment? Probably. He disliked Levenson, but as an experienced agent, he probably had a lot to teach a probie like Finn.

On the other hand, he liked Noah and his story did sound plausible. Even though he was caught climbing into a secure building, and five hundred thousand dollars worth of precious gems were missing. If the kid had stolen the gems where were they? Plus In Finn's opinion, there wasn't a teenage boy alive who possessed his full cognitive ability when there was the possibility of sex.

Finn didn't have enough of the facts to form a conclusion about the case. He didn't know how long it had taken to apprehend Noah once the alarm was triggered. He also didn't know how thoroughly the crime scene had been searched. And what about this Anna? Was anyone checking out that angle – the one where Noah was telling the truth?

He stuffed some more documents into a file. Only another thousand pieces of paper to go.

****

Finn glanced at his watch, ten o'clock in the morning, and he still had a pile of papers a foot high. He stood, massaged his neck, and then arched his back until it popped.

Levenson glanced up from his computer. "The kid's in a holding cell until his mom gets here, I don't want you going near him."

"Like I said earlier, I was just curious." He should apologize. He'd crossed a line, but for some reason he couldn't say the words aloud. Maybe it had something to do with the big stack of filing.

"Didn't you hear curiosity killed the cat?" Nathan leaned back, his legs, and arms spread wide, a posture that implied absolute confidence. It was a pose rarely seen in the workplace, making Finn wonder about its significance. Either Levenson was extremely confident with his role in the FBI, or he had a disproportionate opinion of his own worth.

"We're investigators. Curiosity is in the job description."

Levenson leaned forward. "Listen to me, smartass. I'm the lead agent and you're the underling. You will do what I tell you, when I tell you—got that?"

"Yes sir." Finn resisted the temptation to give him a mock salute. On top of his other shortcomings, the Special Agent didn't seem to have much of a sense of humor. Come to think of it, he didn't seem to have any empathy either. Otherwise, he would consider the possibility that Noah Lewis was a pawn in a bigger scheme.

Finn ached to investigate the kid's story. He wanted to find this girl, Anna, and the diamonds. Where were they? What if Noah was telling the truth? If you worked at a diamond exchange and you wanted to steal some gems, authorities would investigate, unless they already had their guy. So how would… "I do have one question though, and maybe as senior agent you can help me understand the finer points of investigative work?" Finn hoped his butt-kissing technique would make Levenson less confrontational.

"Shoot."

"Did the kid have the diamonds on him?"

"No, I think he stashed them. You should see the tape of him climbing that building. It was like watching a monkey. I reckon he stashed them in a crack or crevice on the outside of the building. We're getting a team with a crane to conduct a search."

"I suppose he has a history of this kind of behavior?" Finn hoped he hadn't stretched the limits of Levenson's patience.

"He doesn't have a record, and there's no indication of him being in trouble at school, but that just means he's never been caught."

"Hi, I'm Lala Atkins from the Operational Technology Division." A tall, slim woman with remarkable deep set, hazel-green eyes, smiled at Finn, revealing a single dimple on her left cheek.

Finn held out his hand. "Nice to meet you."

"I've been sent to enhance the video from the Wolff diamond robbery."

Finn encased long, slim fingers in a firm shake. Her short, white–blonde hair, and perfect makeup made it impossible to pinpoint her age. She could be anywhere from thirty-five to fifty-nine.

"I'm the special agent assigned to this case." Levenson stood, adjusting his tie.

Lala held out her hand to the agent. "Nice to meet you. I'm new to the New York office. Maybe you can show me where you store the digital files."

"I transferred the data to a memory stick. It's all documented." Levenson put his hands on his hips, puffing his chest, reminding Finn of a rooster.

"Doesn't she need to show her ID?" Finn couldn't put his finger on it, but there was something off about Lala Atkins. It wasn't her hair or makeup, although she was a little more put together than the average computer geek, and older, too. But that was stereotyping, not fact. No, it was something else, something in the shape of her face, and the color of her eyes. It was as if he'd seen her before, but couldn't pinpoint where?

Lala looked in her shoulder bag. "Oh, I have it here somewhere. Let me see."

Levenson glared at Finn, and then smiled at Lala. "No, that won't be necessary."

"We're supposed to wear our ID at all times, but the cord makes my neck itch." She smiled at Levenson.

"Don't worry about it. You couldn't have passed through security without your identification. We'll sign the stick out of evidence, and there's a spare desk in the computer lab you can use." He walked toward the elevators. Lala followed. Finn got a pleasing view of long slim legs. For some reason, he'd rather not examine, he'd always been partial to a woman's slim ankles. Whenever he encountered an attractive lady he was always drawn to the contours of her lower leg, and Lala's were exceptional.

He shivered. What was it about her that made him feel as if ants were crawling down his back? It wasn't a new sensation; he'd felt it before. Normally, when the proverbial shit was about to hit the proverbial fan.
****

Tiny pins of pain stabbed at Finn's feet. He slammed the bottom drawer of the filing cabinet closed. He stood and stretched his legs, hoping to improve his circulation. His stomach growled. He scanned his watch— noon. He would break for lunch at one, that way the afternoon would seem shorter. Yeah right.

Levenson looked up from his computer screen. "The woman from OTD was supposed to come and tell me when she'd finished cleaning the video. It's been a couple of hours. What do you think is keeping her?"

Finn's skin tingled, telling him something wasn't right. "Why don't you call the lab? Perhaps there's a problem."

"Good idea. She might need my assistance." Levenson waggled his eyebrows, and then picked up the phone, dialing the extension. "You have a tech there from OTD. Her name's Lala Atkins. I need to talk to her."

He listened for a moment, and then said, "What do you mean she left? How long ago?"

He hung up the phone without saying goodbye, and looked at Finn. "She left an hour ago."

"Why didn't she contact you once she'd finished the job?"

"No idea." Levenson blinked, and then stared into the distance. "Oh God." He sprinted to the elevator.

Had Nathan signed evidence over to a criminal? Perhaps. There was something about Lala Atkins that made Finn uneasy. Was she a hacker? Had she wiped the evidence in the Diamond District case? Maybe, but why would anyone do that? As far as he could tell, Noah was just a kid, a nobody. Walking into an FBI Building and duping a senior agent required nerve and planning. His gut told him it wasn't something a rank amateur would attempt. Were the people behind the robbery trying to clear Noah? Criminals with a conscience? In Finn's experience there was no such thing. This was complicated, a lot more complicated than a teenager stealing some diamonds. What was Noah Lewis' role in all this? Was he a gullible patsy, a diversion for an organized ring of thieves? Or something else?

A dejected Levenson returned to his desk accompanied by their superior, Supervisory Special Agent Mark Windham, a man who still seemed fit and perceptive despite an impressive amount of grey in his dark, curly hair. "Wasn't there any sign she wasn't the real deal?"

"None." Levenson jutted out his chin in an attempt to look confident.

"There'll be a full inquiry. I've contacted the Department of Justice. They're sending a federal prosecutor. I've also assigned agents to look into security footage to see if we've got this Lala Atkins on camera. There will be repercussions."

Yes, sir," Levenson said, not making eye contact with Finn.

"Lucky for you, a witness has come forward," Windham continued. "She's elderly, and lives in an apartment across the street. Says she saw the whole thing. She's in interview room A. Take her statement. Callaghan I want you there. This'll be a good learning experience for you."

Finn smiled. Finally a reprieve from filing.

"I will do the talking. You are there just to observe. Got it." Levenson said the moment Windham was out of earshot.

Finn kept his mouth shut. But he was beginning to doubt whether Levenson could teach him anything useful. He considered the senior agent to be an obnoxious jerk with the investigative skills of a bunny rabbit on meth.

Interview room A was a comfortable corner office with a panoramic view of Downtown Manhattan. Unlike the grey partitions of the main office, it was decorated in subtle green tones with dark, cherry, wood trim, and reminded Finn of an upscale coffee shop. In the center of the room were four comfortable, matching armchairs, placed facing each other to encourage conversation. The idea being that a comfy witness would be more prone to talk.

"I'm Edna Rush, and you are?" An elderly woman with curly, grey hair used her cane to lever herself out of her seat. She held out a hand encased in a delicate lace glove. Pink framed, coke-bottle glasses dwarfed her face. Everything about her screamed old lady from her shapeless, floral dress, which hung on her thin frame, to her baggy, beige stockings.

"I'm Special Agent Levenson." Nathan smiled, and extended his hand, ignoring Finn.

"It's nice to meet you." She shook hands with the agent, and then eased herself into the seat. "Where do you want me to start?"

"Tell us, in your own words, what you saw, and I'll ask questions as we go." Levenson sat opposite Ms. Rush, grabbing a pen, and paper off the coffee table. Finn remained standing.

"Yesterday morning I saw Mr. Wolff screaming at his niece. I call her his niece, but you gentlemen both know what that means, don't you?" She smiled, tilting her head to the side, a sign of confidence.

Levenson cleared his throat. "You mean his lady friend?"

"Yes, that's right." Her lips turned up at the corners, and her eyebrows sat high, above her glasses, which suggested she was being forthright.

"Do you know her name?"

"No, actually, I don't even know if the man I call Mr. Wolff is really named Wolff. I call him that because he works at Wolff Diamond Merchants, and seems to be in charge."

"Can you describe him?" Levenson placed a pad of paper on his knee, not looking at Ms. Rush.

"Yes, he has a slim build, glasses, and receding hair."

"What color is his hair?" Levenson scribbled notes, still not observing the witness.

"Umm, what little he has is light brown."

"And you saw Mr. Wolff with this woman—"

"They were having an argument. I couldn't hear what it was about—"

"Where were you?"

"I was at my living room window on the fourth floor. I have a chair facing the street so I can sit, and watch—"

"How do you know they were arguing if you were so far away?"

"It's called body language. I'd have thought you'd know all about it."

Finn suppressed a smile.

Nathan glanced up. "Yes, of course, but what about their body language—"

"He hit her."

"He hit her?" Levenson scribbled on the notepad.

"Yes, in the street as brazen as you please. It didn't matter to him that there were witnesses."

"Did anyone else see this assault?" Nathan rubbed the back of his neck. A pacifying behavior.

"I'm sure lots of people saw it, but whether they'll come forward…I just don't know. People—"

"Maybe we should get to the part where you saw the kid climbing the building and stealing the diamonds." Levenson compressed his lips into a thin line.

Finn sighed. Nathan's non-verbal behavior suggested he was frustrated with the witness, which was probably why he was telling her what to say.

"I'm sorry?" Edna blinked.

"You said you witnessed a diamond theft." The Special Agent flattened his tie. A soothing mechanism. He was irritated, and losing patience. Something Finn considered a disastrous mistake. Once a witness sensed you didn't like them they stopped talking, or worse, told you what they thought you wanted to hear.

"Witnessed isn't exactly the right word, dear. I just know it happened," Edna continued.

"You know—"

"Did I tell you my father was in diamonds? He taught me how to spot a fake—"

"What has this got to do with—?"

"Because they're fake."

"What are?"

"Wolff's diamonds."

"I don't understand." Levenson gritted his teeth.

"After Mr. Wolff hit that poor, young thing I decided to check out his store. Any man who'd strike a woman in public is just not to be trusted." She tugged her voluminous skirt over her drooping stockings and then leant forward, as if to share a secret. "His diamonds are fake."

"Fake?" Levenson squeaked.

"Yes, I think you should check his inventory."

"What about the boy who climbed through the window?"

"A boy climbed...I don't know what you're talking about. And I wish you'd stop interrupting. I saw the police cars this morning, and heard there was a theft. I'm telling you Mr. Wolff's *diamonds* can't be stolen because they weren't real in the first place."

"So you think the stolen *diamonds* were fake?" Finn interrupted.

"Yes, that's exactly what I'm saying."

Levenson flattened his tie against his shirt again, and cleared his throat. Another soothing mechanism "Maybe Noah Lewis stole the fakes not knowing—"

"On television the motive is always money. You know—insurance fraud. Which makes sense when you think about it. Wolff sells the real diamonds and receives compensation for the stolen ones."

"But the kid—"

"What kid? Do you mean a child or a young goat?" She pursed her lips and made clicking sounds with her tongue. "I'd have thought an FBI agent would be more precise."

"But he-he-he..." Splotches of red appeared high on Levenson's cheeks. "You're lying—"

"Thank you for coming forward. We'll be in touch if we need further information." Finn interrupted before Levenson could harangue her.

Once again, she used her cane to struggle to a standing position. "Do you know I worked my whole life in my father's jewelry store? You can always tell—"

"Let me walk you out." Finn opened the door to the office.

"That won't be necessary dear. I'm sure you have important work to do."

Finn pictured his stack of filing. "Not really."

Levenson trailed two steps behind, sulking.

As they approached the elevator, the doors opened and Senior Special Agent Windham stepped out. The agent wasn't paying attention, and almost slammed into Ms. Rush. She sidestepped him without using her cane. It was a nifty move, worthy of an athlete. Well, maybe not an athlete, but at the very least an able-bodied person.

As the elevator doors closed Finn took a long hard look at her legs, and was surprised to see slim, shapely ankles. Remarkable, deep-set hazel-green eyes smiled at him over coke-bottle glasses. The corners of her lips turned up as her smile deepened, revealing a dimple on the left side of her face?

Finn snapped to attention. Where had he seen those eyes?

Damn it, he'd observed Levenson in the interview because the agent had made such a mess of it, but he should have been looking at the witness. Her hair appeared natural. Could it be a wig? Her face wasn't overly wrinkled. Why did she appear old? Her movements were stiff, and her shoulders hunched. But those things were an affect. Any decent actor could mimic those characteristics.

He slapped a hand to his head, and then grabbed Levenson's arm. "We have to stop her. She's Lala Atkins."

"Don't be ridiculous." Levenson tugged out of Finn's grasp, and then headed back to his desk. How had a jerk like him managed to become an FBI agent? Officially the case was assigned to Levenson. Finn had no input, but he needed to know, even if it was just to satisfy his own curiosity. He hesitated for a moment, and then headed for the stairs.

****

Finn stepped outside, squinting against the bright afternoon sun. He spotted Edna Rush on a bench across from the entrance to the federal building. Was she waiting for him? He dodged oncoming traffic as he crossed Duane Street. "Do you mind if I sit down?"

Intelligent eyes narrowed, assessing him, and then she nodded.

"Who is Noah to you?"

She'd taken off her glasses, making it easy to gauge her response to his question. Her eyes widened, just for a moment, and then gave a small squint, telling him she was surprised by his question, and had a negative response to it.

"He's related to you, isn't he? Let me guess, your grandson?"

"I beg your pardon. I told you I've never been married." She sounded indignant, but Finn wasn't fooled.

"There's a familial resemblance. You have the same color eyes, and you both have a single dimple on the left side."

"That's hardly conclusive—"

"Let me tell you what I think happened. You heard Noah was in trouble. Then you walked into the FBI headquarters as bold as brass, claiming to be Lala Atkins with Operational Technology Division. You destroyed the video evidence of Noah climbing that building. How am I doing so far?"

"You tell an interesting story, Agent Callaghan, but it's just that—a story."

Finn shrugged and continued. "Then you adopted the persona of Edna Rush, who just happens to live across the street from where the robbery occurred. But I bet if I checked I'd find no one in that building knows you."

"Really, you do have a fertile imagination."

"Yeah, I do, which is why I think someone, probably Wolff, heard about Noah, and realized how useful his talent for free climbing could be. But the problem is Noah's not a criminal, he has no history of criminal activity, and he's never been in trouble at school. I think Wolff persuaded Anna to entice him. She convinced him she was in love with him and wanted to have sex with him. But Noah was always a diversion. He triggered the alarm when he climbed through the window, while Wolff made off with the diamonds. Real or fake it doesn't matter. My guess, they were gone before Noah started his climb."

"An inside job." The corners of her mouth turned up in a genuine smile.

"That was why you materialized as Edna Rush, wasn't it? So you could point the finger at Wolff."

"I just told you the truth."

"The woman Noah calls Anna Zingel is either Wolff's girlfriend or employed by him in some capacity. Maybe Wolff beats her, maybe he doesn't. It's hard to say what's real and what's not. But I do know Noah climbed that building, and entered through the third floor window because he told me."

"It's your word against his. Where's your proof?"

"Proof of what? Noah free-climbing, or the fact that you, and Lala Atkins are one, and the same?"

"It doesn't matter because you can't prove any of it."

"If I checked would I find your fingerprints on file?"

"My prints aren't in any database."

"Who are you?"

"You don't have the clearance to know who I am. You came out here alone without the other agent because you think Noah is innocent. Don't you?"

"No, I'm here alone because this is my second day on the job, and Agent Levenson doesn't believe you and Lala Atkins are the same person. By the way, how do you know my name?"

"Because we were introduced by—"

"No, special agent Levenson never introduce me, not to Edna Rush or Lala Atkins."

She ignored his accusation. "Noah's innocent, you know. And once this is over he'll be leaving for Montana. He can climb mountains there. Maybe you should relocate to Montana, too, Agent Callaghan. You have friends there."

"How do you know about my friends?" He hadn't mentioned his buddies from basic training to her, or anyone else. They talked on the phone from time to time, and sent each other Christmas cards, but he hadn't seen them in years.

She smiled. "Sonny, I like you. You're too good to be stuck here working with an idiot like Levenson. You should think about relocating to a field station. The politics of a big city like New York aren't for you."

Finn stood. "I can't let you leave. You impersonated a federal agent, and tampered with evidence. I have to arrest you."

She stood, shoulders back, no longer clinging to her Edna Rush persona. "I have a riddle for you. Who do retired spies spy on?"

"Callaghan, what the hell are you doing out here?" Levenson stood a few yards in front of him, on the sidewalk.

Finn stepped toward his mentor. "We have to arrest this woman. She's Lala Atkins, and Edna Rush."

"This again?" Nathan rolled his eyes.

"Yes, they're the same person."

"That's not possible."

"It is, and if you looked at her." Finn turned, and pointed to the bench, but she was gone. "Where the hell did she go?" He spun around.

The city sidewalk was choked with pedestrians.

He pointed to the end of the block, where Duane met Broadway. "You go that way."

Levenson obeyed, dodging people as he ran.

Finn sprinted to the other end of the street, but there was no sign of her.

"Who is she?" Levenson asked as they retraced their steps back to Federal plaza.

"A retired spy, maybe."

"Are you serious?" Nathan frowned, and raised an eyebrow, a look that suggested Finn was insane, and maybe he was right.

But one question really bothered Finn; how had she known about his friends? They served in the military; one was even in the Special Forces. The Department of Justice had done a full background check when the FBI recruited him, and had researched all his associates. For her to know that much about him suggested she'd done some deep digging and accessed secure files.

He made his way through security, stopping to wait for an elevator. All he could do was tell Supervisory Special Agent Windham his suspicions, and let the senior agent deal with it.

Levenson stood next to him. "You've had a break, now it's time to get back to your filing."

"I'm putting in for a transfer to Montana." He must be insane. He'd just been assigned to New York, why would he want to relocate? But the minute the words were out of his mouth he knew it was the right decision.

"Why?" Levenson scrunched his face, furrowing his eyebrows.

"I hear they have less paperwork."

As a bonus I've included the first chapter from my upcoming novel Sun Seeker, which is due to be released in 2017

CHAPTER ONE

Marie Wilson fanned the tiny flame, trying to get the kindling to ignite before she froze to death. Damn, January in Montana was cold. Despite her discomfort, a pulse of excitement zinged through her. She stood, blew on her frozen fingers and stamped her feet trying to get some feeling in her toes. The forecast predicted a temperature of minus ten Fahrenheit, with the possibility of a blizzard. But that was what she wanted—to test her solar panel in the worst conditions possible.

A flame sparked to life. She suppressed the urge to jump up and down and do a dance for joy. Instead, she yanked on the handle that operated the flue. A blast of cold air from the chimney told her it was open. Very carefully, so as not to extinguish the flame, she added a log to the burning kindling, and then another, and was gratified when they ignited, too. There was something very primal, and comforting about sitting in front of a fire, watching the orange blaze glow.

When she'd rented the remote log cabin with no running water, and no heat, she hadn't imagined lighting a fire at four in the morning. The place did come with a generator, but she had chosen not to hook it up – not yet anyway.

She'd attempted to sleep in her thermal long johns, but the frigid temperature had forced her to wear her coat and boots. She fingered her socks as they hung on the back of a wooden chair. They were still wet. It was her own fault. She'd shed her boots and then walked through a puddle of melted snow. By the front door, no less, where one would expect the floor to be damp. Of course, most people would've remembered to pack extra socks, but she wasn't most people. She was a scientist on the verge of a breakthrough. Tomorrow, if everything went as planned, she would validate her work and gain the respect of the scientific community.

She glanced around the musty cottage, which was really just one room. At the back was a counter for food preparation, a hand-pump sink, and a hot plate. A wooden table stood near the door, and in front of the stove sat an oak-framed futon couch. The owner had described the small house as rustic, which she assumed was another word for neglected. Maybe it was pretty in the summer, but when the snow sat five feet high outside her front door, and the wind whistled through a cracked window frame, it was just miserable.

She returned to the mildewed couch. There was one blanket, which stank of mold, rendering it unusable. Not that she needed a comforter because her attempt to get some much-needed sleep had proved futile. She was too excited.

To reach the cabin, she had flown to Hope Falls, Montana that morning, rented a car, and survived a white-knuckle drive on icy, country roads. Thank God the owner had shoveled the driveway, otherwise her little orange rental car would not have made it through the snow.

She planned to do some preparation for the tests but dusk had come earlier than anticipated. Had the extreme cold damaged the prototype? She pulled her hair into a ponytail and then dragged her backpack across the floor. Unfolding the plastic, gold, indented sheet, she checked for any signs of damage. Some plastics became brittle at low temperatures. That was something she would have to consider for future models. She inspected the tablet cover that protected the transformer, but there was no way to tell if it was damaged until she hooked it up.

The little house might be miserable, but it was the perfect location to test her solar panel. Tomorrow she would rewire the generator, power the cottage, and prove her hypotheses correct. Professor Hargreaves from Montana Tech would join her around lunchtime. His recommendation would go a long way toward her gaining recognition for her work.

She closed her eyes, letting the crackle of the flames sooth her. A rustle at the door captured her attention. Something was out there. She'd seen animal tracks when she'd arrived. Had a deer wondered close to the cabin? There it was again, a sound almost like footsteps crunching on the snow. Could it be a bear? No, they hibernated through the winter.

The crack of splintering wood as her front door crashed open propelled Marie to her feet, heart pounding. A scream lodged in her throat as four men burst in, filling the tiny space. She raced to the fireplace, and grabbed the poker. This couldn't be happening. Just moments before she had lit a fire, and now there were men in her house. It must be a mistake, and they would apologize, and leave.

A handsome blond-haired man led the way, heading toward her. Two burly men with dark, short-cropped hair, who could be twins, followed. They moved to the back of the room, near the sink.

The last man had unkempt, sandy-colored hair. He wore a crumpled, hooded camouflage jacket and baggy grey pants. A long scar ran across one side of his face. It started at his ear and lead to his beard, parting it with a jagged white line. His pale eyes, which glowed in the flickering firelight, were dead and emotionless. Everything about him suggested he was coiled and ready to strike, from his shoulders, which were tight and tense, to his hands that were balled into fists and positioned at his waist, poised to attack. Without saying a word, he nodded at the poker in her hand and shook his head, silently telling her to drop her weapon.

She let it fall to the ground, sensing that any attempt to fight him would be futile. "You can take the money. I don't have—"

"Shut up," the handsome blond barked. A vein on his forehead bulged as he scowled.

Her heart hammered against her ribs, as her knees threatened to buckle. She prayed they would take what they want and leave.

Handsome stood in front of her, and placed the barrel of his handgun between her eyes. "Tell us where it is."

"What, the fuck, are you doing?" The man with the scar strolled over and stood next to her. In her peripheral vision, she could make out his intense, pale, lifeless eyes. The scar, those dead eyes and his demeanor gave her the impression he was intimate with danger and death. *A Killer.*

He leaned close to her face so his warm breath touched her cheek. "This is all wrong."

A small squeal emanated from her throat. He was too close. Too scary.

"What do you mean? Our intel is good." The vein on Handsome's forehead throbbed to life.

With one finger, Killer nudged the pistol away from her head. "First, how can she tell us where it is when she's too frightened to talk?"

Handsome shrugged and holstered his weapon. Then he smiled, revealing perfect white teeth.

Marie released a huge breath. She needed to do something, but couldn't focus, couldn't form a coherent thought.

"Second," Killer continued, "what do we really know about this situation?"

Handsome sneered. "You were in the army. You know how it is. We don't make the decisions. We follow orders."

"And what exactly are our orders?" Killer asked, his voice low, calm and threatening.

"We're to retrieve what was stolen, and eliminate the girl."

There had to be a misunderstanding. She was a *scientist*, not someone who needed to be *eliminated.*

"Does she seem like a threat to you? Someone we should murder? She smells like"—Killer sniffed her hair—"coconut."

She resisted the temptation to pull away, not wanting to attract more attention. She had to concentrate, control her fear, and get out of here in one piece.

A movement caught her eye as the two other men, the musclemen, stepped closer.

"What are your plans?" Killer turned his nose into her hair and sniffed again, but the question was directed to the others. "Are you planning to use her before you kill her."

She stepped to the side, trying to put some distance between her and the scarred man with the dead eyes, but he grabbed her arm and tugged her toward him.

She wanted to fight, but her muscles were so weak they might as well have been made of string cheese.

"Retrieving the prototype is number one on my to-do list, and then if these two want to have some fun, I won't stop them," Handsome said.

She swallowed bile, suppressing the urge to vomit. She gulped in shallow breaths. They were going to rape and kill her. *Oh God.* Her vision blurred, and her ears rang. No, she would not faint. If she lost consciousness, she wouldn't be able to defend herself.

Killer tightened his grasp on her arm, causing her to wince. She inhaled, held her breath, and then exhaled. She repeated the process, forcing herself to concentrate on the men.

Killer's gaze flickered to the two bruisers and then back to Handsome. "Either way she's going to die? Those are our orders?"

Handsome nodded. "Do you have a problem?"

Killer ignored the question. He released her arm and hooked her chin, forcing her to stare into his pale dead eyes. "These men think you have a stolen prototype. Do you know what they're talking about?"

Cold beads of fear dribbled down her spine. She pointed a shaky hand to her backpack, which sat on the floor next to the futon.

Handsome flipped the bag upside-down, emptying its contents. Out dropped her wallet, a hairbrush, her smart phone, a pen, a tampon, a memory stick, the solar array, the power transformer, and a lint-covered collection of dimes and nickels.

"It's not here," Handsome threw her bag across the room toward the fireplace. Then kicked the futon. The heavy couch moved back a couple of inches. "You must have more clothes. Where's your suitcase?"

Marie pointed to a small carry-on parked by the front door. The Twins tore it apart, scattering her clothing about the room.

"What sort of prototype are you looking for?" Killer stepped forward, placing himself between her and Handsome.

"A solar panel, and a gizmo." Handsome scrubbed a hand over his face.

"A gizmo? Seriously? You don't fucking know what we're looking for."

Handsome rolled his eyes. "I'm looking for a prototype of a solar panel."

"A solar panel? That's not going to fit in her bag, now is it?"

Marie took a step toward the door.

Killer glanced over his shoulder and shook his head, stopping her in her tracks.

****

How, the hell, had he gotten himself embroiled with this fucked-up assignment? This was David Quinn's first day on the job, and it looked like it would be his last because he wasn't going to execute a woman, especially not a pretty little thing who wore pink long johns and smelt of coconut. Not that he planned to kill anyone. Marshall Portman, the president of Public Domain Energy, had asked David to help retrieve some stolen property, but there had been no mention of murder, at least not to him.

The woman looked ready to bolt, but she needed to wait. If she took off now, the other three members of his detail would chase her down. Inside the cabin he could immobilize them and control the situation. Once outside, they would be harder to overpower, and the chances of her getting away, unscathed, diminished.

Her long, brown hair stuck out at odd angles as it escaped her ponytail. Her coat had fallen open, revealing a curvaceous body clad in tight-fitting thermal underwear. Never mind lacy lingerie, the smooth cotton clinging to her breasts did a number on him. Her shape and those soft brown eyes converged into a mind-blowing, sexy-as-hell combination, which made her position here even more dangerous.

The biggest problem was his team leader, Brad Harper, whom David secretly called Pretty-boy, was an idiot. The guy looked like he would be more at home modeling clothes in a magazine than operating a team of ex-military personnel who'd been sent to recover a stolen prototype before it could be sold on the black market.

David eyed the two chimps that made up the other members of the four-man team. Alex and Shane, the twins. Both were big and muscular with dark hair. Alex had a scar across his chin.

Both rested a hand on the weapon in their shoulder holsters as if they were getting ready for a quick draw. Did they see him as a threat? They should. Everything had gone to hell the moment they'd stormed through the door. Brad didn't have a clue...about anything, and the chimps seemed more intent on rape than retrieving a stolen solar panel.

Shane, the one without a scar, favored his left leg, possibly a bum knee. Alex took his hand off his revolver and absentmindedly massaged his shoulder. David stored the information away.

He strolled to Brad, who stood at the couch rummaging through the contents of her backpack. Glancing over Pretty-boy's shoulder, David said, "Why are you still looking through her things?"

"Look at this frou-frou shit." Brad held up a gold plastic sheet, which was about a yard in diameter. "What do women use this stuff for?"

"Does it matter? A solar panel is not going to fit in a backpack. Are you sure she has it?"

"Yeah."

David studied the girl. She'd backed up until her butt was against the table. "What's your name?"

"M-M-Marie." She was scared, but holding it together—just.

"Marie what?"

"W-Wilson, Dr. Marie Wilson."

He turned to Brad. "Is that the name you're looking for?"

"I think so?"

"You think so." What kind of a dumb-shit answer was that?

Brad held up his smartphone. "These are the GPS coordinates, see?"

David didn't bother to look. He didn't care if they had a signed order from the Pope. He wasn't murdering anyone.

"Alex, Shane, make her talk," Brad ordered as he jerked his semi automatic, a Glock 19, from his belt and slid the safety off.

The chimps smiled.

Alex strolled toward Marie, unzipping his pants.

Shit.

Marie's lips trembled. She blinked, unable to tear her gaze away from the two meatheads closing in on her. She fumbled behind her, reaching for the car keys, which lay just out of range.

Brad aimed his gun, at David's chest. Without thinking, David pushed the Glock to the side and stepped sideways, out of the line of sight. He then grasped the weapon, and twisted it, up and back, toward Brad until he relinquished the gun. Using his right elbow, he jabbed Brad hard in the nose. Pretty boy screamed as his cartilage snapped.

David fired the Glock at the ceiling above the table. Chunks of wood rained down on the chimps, stopping them.

He stepped away from Brad, gripping the semi-automatic. "I'm all for you guys getting your property back, but I can't let you harm her."

Marie darted to her jumble of possessions on the couch and stuffed them in her backpack.

"What are you? A knight in fucking armor?" Brad shrieked, clutching both hands to his bloody nose.

"I'm a soldier, not a rapist, and definitely not a murderer. I don't want to be part of this." He sounded tired even to his own ears. He wanted everything to stop, the operations, the missions, the fighting, and most of all the death. Taking a position with Public Domain Energy had been a mistake. He saw that now. All he had to do was disentangle himself from this mess, quit his job, and go on his way. "Okay, here's what's going to happen—"

Before he could finish, Marie ran out of the cabin.

David stared after her. "Shit, she'll freeze to death. You know what you're looking for isn't in her pack, right?"

Brad nodded, still clasping his nose.

"Then search the rest of the house. She obviously doesn't have your stolen prototype on her. If you find it, great. I'm outta here." He grabbed Marie's car keys off the table and marched out into the frigid night.

Sun Seeker is due to be released in 2017

Thank you for purchasing this publication from Viceroy Press
If you enjoyed the story, we would appreciate your letting others know.
For other wonderful stories by Marlow, please visit her website at
www.marlowkelly.com or her Amazon Page at:
http://www.amazon.com/Marlow-Kelly/e/B00MZE72CS

For questions or more information contact Marlow at
marlow@marlowkelly.com
Like Marlow on Facebook: https://www.facebook.com/marlowkelly/
And Follow Marlow on Twitter: https://twitter.com/want2write
And Pinterest: https://www.pinterest.com/Marlowkelly14/
To receive the latest news about Marlow's new releases sign up for her
Newsletter: http://eepurl.com/bnUBqn

Made in the USA
Middletown, DE
13 September 2019